HAMMOND PUBLIC SCHOOLS
Corrective Reading

TITLE I

To Momo
on her
eighth
birthday

Pic Bk   SBN 670–05031–8
Library of Congress catalog card number: 58–14714

2   3   4   5   74   73   72

UMBRELLA

BY TARO YASHIMA

New York: The Viking Press

Copyright © 1958 by Taro Yashima. All rights reserved. Viking Seafarer edition issued in 1970 by The Viking Press, Inc. Distributed in Canada by The Macmillan Company of Canada Limited. Printed in U.S.A.

 *Haru* (Spring)

Momo is the name of a little girl
who was born in New York.
The word *Momo* means "the peach" in Japan
where her father and mother used to live.

2

On her third birthday
Momo was given two presents—
red rubber boots and an umbrella!
They pleased her so much
that she even woke up that midnight
to take another look at them.

 *Natsu* (Summer)

Unfortunately
it was still Indian summer,
and the sun was bright.
Every morning
Momo asked her mother,
who used to take her
to the nearby nursery school,
"Why the rain doesn't fall?"
The answer was always the same:
"Wait, wait; it will come."

6

One morning
Momo was more impatient than ever,
because the sun
was brighter than ever.
But, strangely enough,
a splendid idea made her jump up
when she was watching
the sunshine in her milk glass.
"I need my umbrella.
The sunshine bothers my eyes!"
But her mother said,
"You know you can enjoy the sunshine
better without the umbrella.
Let's keep it for a rainy day."

8

Next morning
Momo was still unhappy,
because she still
could not use her umbrella.
But, strangely enough,
another idea made her jump up
when she was watching
the people on the street.
"I certainly need my umbrella today!
The wind must bother my eyes!"
But her mother said,
"The wind might blow your umbrella away.
Let's keep it for a rainy day."

 *Ame* (Rain)

It was many, many days later
that finally the rain fell.
Momo was wakened
by her mother's voice—
"Get up! Get up! What a surprise for you!"

Momo did not stop to wash her face.
She even pulled the boots
onto her bare feet—
she was so excited.

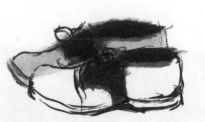

The pavement was all wet and new—
doodling she had drawn yesterday
was not there any more.
Instead, raindrops
were jumping all over,
like the tiny people dancing.

The street was crowded and noisy,
but she whispered to herself,
"I must walk straight,
like a grown·up·lady!"

On the umbrella,
raindrops made a wonderful music
she never had heard before—

> *Bon polo*
> *bon polo*
> *ponpolo ponpolo*
> *ponpolo ponpolo*
> *bolo bolo ponpolo*
> *bolo bolo ponpolo*
> *boto boto ponpolo*
> *boto boto ponpolo*

The rain did not stop all day long.
Momo watched it at times while she was playing
the games at the nursery school.

She did not forget her umbrella
when her father came
to take her home.
She used to forget
her mittens or her scarf so easily—
but not her umbrella.

The street was crowded and noisy,
but she whispered to herself,
"I must walk straight,
like a grown-up lady!"

On her umbrella, the raindrops
made the wonderful music—

> *Bon polo*
> *bon polo*
> *ponpolo ponpolo*
> *ponpolo ponpolo*
> *bolo bolo ponpolo*
> *bolo bolo ponpolo*
> *boto boto ponpolo*
> *boto boto ponpolo*

all the way home.

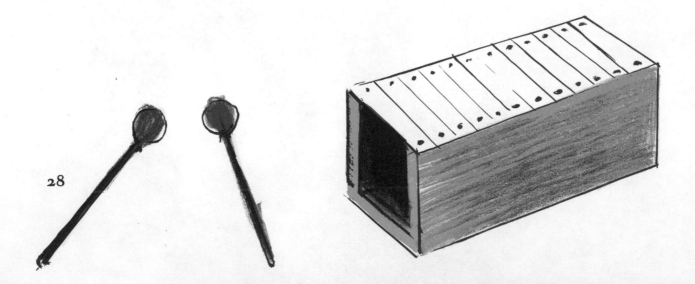

Momo (Peach)

Momo is a big girl now,
and this is a story
she does not remember at all.

Does she remember or not,
it was not only the first day in her life
that she used her umbrella,
it was also the first day in her life
that she walked alone,
without holding either
her mother's or her father's hand.